Eliott the Penguin

Written by **Kris Lee**   Illustrated by **Cary Lamb Jr**

This book belongs to:

_____

Eliott the Penguin wakes up to sunshine and a heart full of gratitude.

"Good morning, world! I'm so happy from that good night's sleep and I'm ready to start my day!"

He jumps out of bed, takes a deep morning stretch. He is excited to start his day.

"I love getting ready for the day. I'm so thankful for this awesome backpack to help carry my books and snacks. It has strawberry ice cream on it, my favorite!"

Eliott walks to school bundled up, with his red mittens and thick red hat. He stops to say hi to Mr. Whale and ask about his day.

"Would you like anything from the store, Mr. Whale? I'm headed there after school."

"Actually," Mr. Whale responds, "I would enjoy some tasty fruit."

Eliott replies, "I would love to help out! I'll bring some by this afternoon."

Eliott gets to school, sits in the front row, and pays attention in class. He makes sure to ask for help from his teachers and peers because he wants to be the very best student he can be.

"I love learning!" exclaims Eliott.

After school, Eliott walks through the halls and signs up to bake cookies for the bake sale to raise money for penguins in need.

"I am thankful that I can help bake cookies to help raise money for penguin families. I know how important family is."

Eliott rides his bike to the store to get Mr. Whale's fruit. He picks up fresh blueberries and a few biscuits.

"I'll pick up an extra tasty treat so Mr. Whale will be pleasantly surprised."

He brings Mr. Whale his blueberries and some sweet biscuits. Mr. Whale is surprised and grateful. Eliott drops off the treats with a happy heart and heads home.

At home, Eliott starts baking cookies.
He smiles as he puts on his cooking apron,
starts prepping the cookies, and whistles
while he bakes.

Eliott loves to dance in the kitchen.

"I love the way cookies smell. My mom will be so pleased when she gets home. She will see I've saved her a few cookies to enjoy with her tea."

After packing up the cookies, he goes to meet with his friend, Mr. Seal. They take a walk in the neighborhood and Eliott listens to Mr. Seal, who isn't having the best day.

Mr. Seal feels self-conscious because he thinks he's too big and slow to try out for the hockey team. But he really wants to. Eliott listens and encourages him to go for it.

He gives Mr. Seal encouragement and support to try out. Eliott is a good listener. He gives Mr. Seal a hug and tells him, "You are good enough."

After saying goodbye to Mr. Seal, Eliott says to himself, "I'm so thankful for great friends. I am a good listener and I help the ones I love in any way I can."

On the way home, Eliott sees Mrs. Gull. He says, "Hi, Mrs. Gull, what a pleasure to see you! Why aren't you flying? I usually don't see you walking."

Mrs. Gull says, "My tote bag tore and the plants I had fell out. I am still far from home and getting a bit tired, but I love these plants, so I'll walk them back to my nest."

"Well, Mrs. Gull, I always keep a needle and thread in my bag. I'll patch up the hole for you!"

Eliott takes out the needle and thread, sews up the hole, and gives the bag back to Mrs. Gull. She is so grateful. She thanks him and flies home with her plants.

Eliott looks up to Mrs. Gull in the sky, waves, and smiles. "I'm thankful my mom spent time with me and showed me how to sew. It allowed me to help someone else."

Eliott returns home to his family. They all sit down for dinner.

They're having homemade pho, his favorite!

He slurps up the noodles, eats all of his vegetables, and grabs the bowl with both fins and gulps down the broth. He sits back with a satisfied smile, rubbing his belly.

"I love and appreciate tasty food. I am thankful for warm, homemade meals made with love. I love enjoying meals with my family."

Eliott helps his family clean up from dinner and tidy up the house. Then he washes up, brushes his teeth, and gets ready for bed.

Before bed, Eliott takes time to write in his gratitude journal. "I am grateful I have the chance every day to be a good friend, a good student, a good neighbor, and a good son. I can't wait to get up and be my best self tomorrow!"

Eliott's mission is to make the world a better place with his smile, attitude, and spirit.

Eliott goes to sleep, happy and fulfilled.

The End

Eliott loved sharing his story with you!

Now it's your turn to share in your gratitude journal.

Write down three things you are grateful for today:

1. _____

2. _____

3. _____

What are three acts of kindness that you can do for someone today?

1. _____

2. _____

3. _____

What qualities make you a good friend?

1. _____

2. _____

3. _____

What are three dreams you have for yourself when you grow up?

1. _____

2. _____

3. _____

What is your favorite healthy snack?

_____

What is your favorite animal?

_____

Thanks for reading my book. I worked
hard to make it great for you.

I love you.

See you in Antarctica!

Love,
Eliott

Made in the USA
Middletown, DE
23 January 2021

32251985R00029